Tess
&
Melanie Fullerling

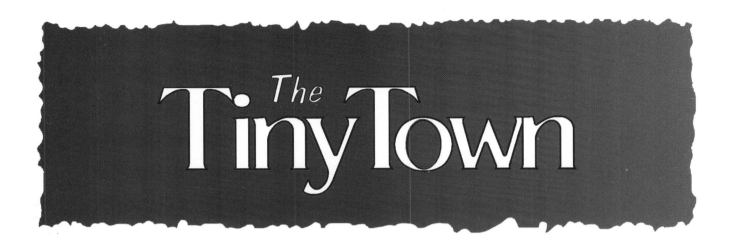

The Tiny Town

Written by Melanie Friedersdorf
Illustrated by Cheryl Biddix

Peaceful Village Publishing
Orlando, Florida

Printed in the United States of America
by Walsworth Publishing Company

1st Printing, 1997

ISBN 0-9658061-7-0
Library of Congress Catalog Card Number: 97-92618

Cover design and page layout by Rob Bullock.

The text of this book is set in Arial font.
The original illustrations are watercolor and pen & ink.

For my parents, Frank and Patricia,
who live sometimes in the mountains
and sometimes by the shore of the sea.
-M.F.

For my coloring crew of nephews,
A.J., Josh and tiny Thor.
-C.L.B.

You are light for all the world.
A town that stands on a hill cannot be hidden.
Matthew 5:14
(Revised English)

There was a tiny town tucked between the mountains and the shore of the sea where all of the buildings were painted their own special color.

2

There were houses the color of pink bubble gum and lime sherbet and the bright blue of the sky, and shops painted like green apples and strawberry milkshakes. The colors were delicious - and unique.

The tiny townspeople knew each building by its special color; and every home, shop, school, church and office was a different hue. The owner of each building was very proud of its color. The tiny town was hundreds of years old, and all of the buildings were splashed with a new coat of pretty paint every few years in exactly the same color.

.5

The master painter and his colorful crew spent their days repainting the buildings. The master painter was also the master mixer and he was the only person in the tiny town who knew the recipe for each building's paint color.

The master painter's home was built on the side of a mountain above the tiny town. His house was lavender and looked quite lovely next to the green grass on the mountainside. Inside the master painter's house all of the paints and recipes for mixing were stored.

It was a full-time job for the master mixer and his colorful crew to keep the buildings painted in their own unique colors. Each morning he would mix the paint in his lovely lavender house, load his cart, and ride down the mountainside to the tiny town to begin painting with his colorful crew.

The sunshine yellow house was always painted sunshine yellow, which was different than daffodil yellow. The sea blue school always got a new coat of sea blue paint; and the bubble gum pink shop was repainted exactly the same shade of bubble gum pink, and was not to be confused with sunset pink.

The winter of the big snow, flakes fell for twenty-two straight days. The snow was as high as the rooftops and, for a few days, the tiny town was mostly white.

When the snow stopped, the sun shined brightly on the mountainside and the sea and the tiny town. The days grew warm. The snow melted quickly.

And an avalanche began.

Snowballs rolled down the mountainside. And, as they rolled, they grew bigger and bigger and rounder and rounder. One especially big snow ball was rolling at exceptional speed. And, in its path, was the home of the master painter!

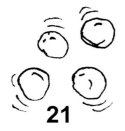

Fortunately, the master painter was in town with his colorful crew when the biggest and roundest snowball of all rolled into his house, turning it into a pile of no-longer-lovely lavender sticks!

Inside the once lovely lavender house, the colorful cans of paint had tipped over, and paint began racing down the mountainside. Rivers of red and green and blue, and streams of fuschia and turquoise and purple ran down to the tiny town and splashed on the buildings.

The tiny townspeople ran out of their homes and into the streets to watch. Their eyes grew big and round and their mouths hung open as they witnessed their tiny town being transformed before them.

The sunshine yellow house was now grass green. The sea blue school turned into a lemon yellow school, and the shop which had been bubble gum pink was now navy blue.

The tiny townspeople gathered in the center of the town. Then, together, they marched up the green mountainside to find the master painter and order him to paint their buildings the colors they had been for hundreds of years.

27

They found the master painter perched atop the pile of lavender sticks which had earlier been his lovely lavender house. He held his head in his hands.

The tiny townspeople began shouting at the master painter to paint their homes and shops immediately. They all argued about whose building should be painted first, and they each thought that it should be their own.

Their shouts were shrill.
Their cries were chaotic.

And the master painter hung his head lower
and lower.

He simply could not paint their homes and
shops and churches and schools and offices
exactly the same colors that they had been for
hundreds of years. The recipes had been kept
in his once lovely lavender house, which was
no longer lovely and no longer a house.

Tess, who was the tiniest townsperson in the tiny town, looked at the sad face of the master painter. While the tiny townspeople shouted and cried, Tess climbed up into his lap and put her arms around the master painter's neck.

"I'm sorry that your house is broken", she said.

 **33**

The master painter raised his head and a slight smile could be seen on his face.

"Thank you for thinking about me", he replied.

"But how will we restore our tiny town to the beautiful colors it was before? The paint recipes have been lost forever."

Tess turned and looked down the mountainside at the tiny town. The sun was bouncing off of the lemon yellow school. The navy blue shop seemed to be floating on the sea beyond it; and the grass green shop was exactly the same color as the grass on the mountainside. The tiny town was an explosion of rainbow colors.

"But", she said, "the new colors are beautiful."

Tess' tiny voice was heard above the shouts and cries of the angry townspeople. As they became still and looked down at the tiny town with its greens and yellows and blues and fuschias, they, too, realized that the tiny town was truly beautiful wearing its new colors.

The Tiny Town is Cheryl Biddix's first book for children. In the Orlando advertising agency where she works, Cheryl is known for her clever, illustrated office memos. She loves her hometown, Winter Park, Florida.

Melanie Friedersdorf is the author of the children's picture book, *Where Do Falling Stars Go?* and the founder of Peaceful Village Publishing. She is happy to call Orlando, Florida her home.

The mission of Peaceful Village Publishing is to produce quality books for children; to educate children on the process of writing, illustrating and publishing books; and to provide children with a vision to pursue their dreams and opportunities to be involved as authors themselves.

Where Do Falling Stars Go? by Melanie Friedersdorf is a picture book for children. The rhyming verses and repetition are ideal for emerging and new readers. A 48-page book filled with colorful and simple artwork.

ISBN #0-9658061-6-2; Library of Congress Catalog Card #97-92197

ORDERING INFORMATION

(QTY)   ($)

_____   *The Tiny Town* @ $16.00 per book   _____

_____   *Where Do Falling Stars Go?* @ $14.95 per book   _____

_____   6% sales tax for Florida residents only   _____

_____ $1.75 shipping and handling per book   _____

                       TOTAL enclosed   _____

Name and address to which book(s) should be sent:

_____

_____

_____

Make check payable to Peaceful Village Publishing
and mail with order form to:

Peaceful Village Publishing
P.O. Box 547831
Orlando, FL 32854

This page may be duplicated.

Where Do Falling Stars Go? by Melanie Friedersdorf is a picture book for children. The rhyming verses and repetition are ideal for emerging and new readers. A 48-page book filled with colorful and simple artwork. ISBN #0-9658061-6-2; Library of Congress Catalog Card #97-92197

ORDERING INFORMATION

(QTY)   ($)

_____   *The Tiny Town* @ $16.00 per book   _____

_____   *Where Do Falling Stars Go?* @ $14.95 per book   _____

_____   6% sales tax for Florida residents only   _____

_____ $1.75 shipping and handling per book   _____

                       TOTAL enclosed   _____

Name and address to which book(s) should be sent:

_____
_____
_____

Make check payable to Peaceful Village Publishing
and mail with order form to:

Peaceful Village Publishing
P.O. Box 547831
Orlando, FL 32854

This page may be duplicated.